P9-DDN-489

For Christy Ottaviano and her boys, Francis and Vincent
—J. L.

For George and Bette; and for Will, who likes my peas,
and Claire, who likes my tomatoes
—D. P.

Henry Holt and Company, LLC
Publishers since 1866
175 Fifth Avenue
New York, New York 10010
www.HenryHoltKids.com

Henry Holt® is a registered trademark of Henry Holt and Company, LLC.
Text copyright © 2010 by Jonathan London
Illustrations copyright © 2010 by David Parkins
All rights reserved.
Distributed in Canada by H. B. Fenn and Company Ltd.

Library of Congress Cataloging-in-Publication Data
London, Jonathan.
I'm a truck driver / Jonathan London ; illustrated by David Parkins. — 1st ed.
p.   cm.
"Christy Ottaviano Books."
Summary: Simple rhyming text introduces sounds and activities of a wide variety of trucks.
ISBN 978-0-8050-7989-0
[1. Stories in rhyme. 2. Trucks—Fiction.] I. Parkins, David, ill. II. Title. III. Title: I am a truck driver.
PZ8.3.L8433Iam 2010   [E]—dc22   2009009220

First Edition—2010 / Designed by Elizabeth Tardiff
The artist used acrylics on canvas paper to create the illustrations for this book.
Printed in October 2009 in China by Imago USA Inc.,
Dongguan City, Guangdong Province, on acid-free paper. ∞

1 3 5 7 9 10 8 6 4 2

I'M A TRUCK DRIVER

Jonathan London • illustrated by David Parkins

Christy Ottaviano Books
Henry Holt and Company
New York

DISCARDED

SCHENECTADY COUNTY
PUBLIC LIBRARY

I'm a **POWER SHOVEL** operator.
I dig up the land.
I operate the gears
and scoop up the sand.

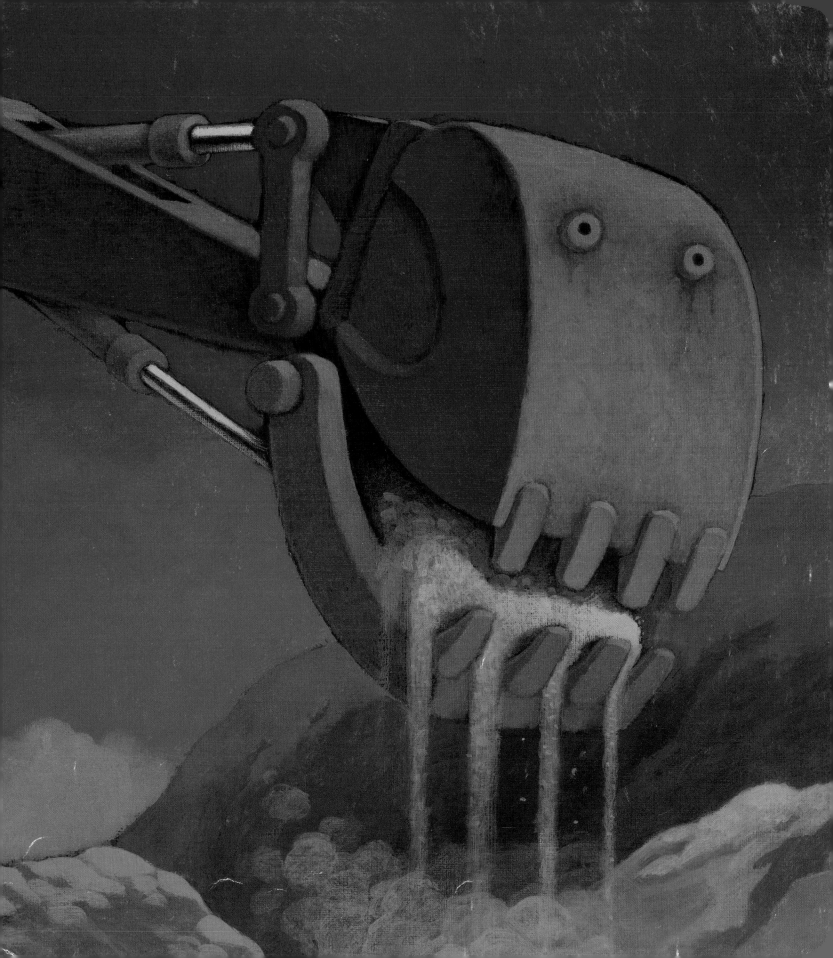

I'm a **CEMENT TRUCK** driver.

Rumble tumble, tumble rumble.

Wet cement in the mixer.

Tumble rumble, rumble tumble.

I'm a big **CRANE** operator.
I lift steel beams high
and build tall buildings
that scrape the blue sky.

I'm a **BULLDOZER** operator.
Growl, grumble, broom!
I'm a big earth mover.
Growl, grumble, broom!

I'm a **STEAMROLLER** driver.
I flatten the tar.
I crush rocks and smooth
new roads for a car.

I'm a **STREET SWEEPER** driver.

Shusha shusha, shusha shusha.

My brushes spin and sweep.

Shusha shusha, shusha shusha.

I'm a **FIRE TRUCK** driver.

That's me behind the wheel.

I race to all the fires.

Hear my siren squeal!

I'm a **SNOWPLOW** driver.
I scoop up the snow.
I scrape the roads clean
so the traffic can flow.

I'm a **TOW TRUCK** driver.

Clinka-vroom, vroom.

I tow smashed cars.

Vroom, vroom, zoom!

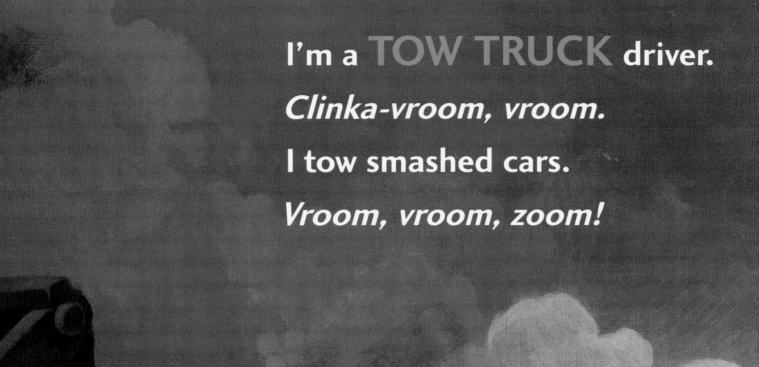

I'm a **COMBINE** operator.

I harvest the grain.

I go row upon row

in sunshine or rain.

I'm a **TRACTOR-TRAILER** driver.

Grum, grum, roar!

I barrel down the highway

Honk, honk, ROAR!